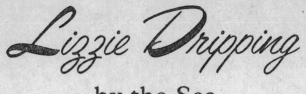

Lizzie Dripping
by the Sea

Helen Cresswell

illustrated by
Faith Jaques

D1324897

British Broadcasting Corporation

For Anna, Angela and Paul
with love and thanks

Published by the British Broadcasting Corporation,
35 Marylebone High Street, London WIM 4AA

ISBN 0 563 12689 2

First published 1974, reprinted 1976

Printed in England by Hazell Watson & Viney Ltd,
Aylesbury, Bucks

Contents

Lizzie Dripping

and the Treasure Hunt

"Have we *got* to take Toby, Mam?" asked Lizzie, pulling on her wellingtons. "You can only go on't roads, wi' pushchair. I want a proper walk.

"Here," said Gramma, waving her umbrella at Lizzie's boots, "*I've* no boots, and shouldn't put 'em on, if I had. Not traipsing across fields, not at my age, thank you."

"Not in *fields*, Gram," said Lizzie. "On't footpaths. You'll be all right. I know *lots* of paths."

"Hark at 'er!" cried Gramma. "*Born* here, my lass, seventy odd years back. More footpaths than there was roads, then. I could show you a few paths, if I was minded."

"Can we leave Toby then, Mam?" asked Lizzie again, and Patty nodded.

"Go on then, pair of you. I don't know which is daftest. And mind that dog don't get filthy wet, like he did yesterday. Comes in here, wags his tail and that's wallpaper all splattered up. Then he wipes hisself across my tights, and he's dry and it's *me* as is wet. You keep an eye on him, Lizzie."

"Oh, I will, Mam," promised Lizzie. "He's ever so good, really."

"Oh aye," said Patty. "I've seen him. Comes bounding up that garden like a blessed stag. Oh well! If he comes home wet he can always stop out till he's dry."

So Lizzie and Gramma set off.

"Not too far," said Gramma as they turned into

Church Lane. "She's right—rain about. Black as Harry's knitting bag over yonder," and she jerked her head in the direction of the church.

Seeing the church must have set off a new train of thought, because she said next: "Lot o' folk I know, in there," meaning the graveyard.

"Someone *I* know, and all," thought Lizzie, meaning the witch.

Gramma crossed Kirk Street and plodded steadily into the churchyard.

"Oh, Gram," cried Lizzie, "you're not going in there now!"

Gramma paid no attention. Instead of taking the little grass path into the sky she marched towards the other gate that led into the graveyard, not more than a few yards from the tomb of the Perfectly Peaceful Posts.

"Oooh!" Lizzie's head went into turmoil. "Witch'll think it's me come to see her, and what if she's there, what if—?"

With relief she saw that the witch was not there—not visibly, at any rate, and in her usual place.

"Hgh!" Gramma stopped and looked about. "Now— where've they put Polly?"

"Polly? Polly Summers, you mean, *Only Sleeping*?" And she saw, horrified, that the witch was there, right behind Gramma. Lizzie shook her head and pulled a face, and the witch grinned and stayed exactly where she was.

"That's her," nodded Gramma, "where is she?"

"She's down there, at bottom end, but it's all nettles and long grass and that. Come on, Gram, let's go for a walk like we said!"

"What's her stone like?" demanded Gramma.

The witch was beckoning now, and Lizzie shook her head again and frowned warningly.

"Lizzie!" snapped Gramma.

"S-sorry, Gram. Oh—her stone—you know, just ordinary. But big—big it is."

"Ah!" cried Gramma triumphantly. "I knew it!

6

It would be. That woman, she'd always to have biggest and best of owt there was going. Always to go one better, that was Polly Summers, and same dead as she was alive, by't look on it."

She paused and stared down the long path through the graveyard and her whole face changed.

"You stop here, Lizzie," she said. "I'm just going down yonder a minute."

Off she went, a sturdy black figure seeming to wade in the long buff tide of grass, and Lizzie thought, "Gone to see Grampa...."

Then she remembered the witch and turned to see if she were still there. She was. "I di'n't *come* to see you," Lizzie told her. "'T'was *Gramma* came. Go away, won't you, and I'll come back later."

"Stop if I want," said the witch huffily.

"But she'll see you!" cried Lizzie.

The witch smiled wickedly and did not answer.

"Oooh—sometimes I get fair *sick* o' you!" cried Lizzie then.

"Hoity toity!" reproved the witch. She wagged a finger. "Hoity toity! You that *brought* me here, remember, in the first place!"

"You don't seem to *realise*!" went on Lizzie. "'S'all right for you—all you've to do is flit about all day, spelling, and that! *Live* in't graveyard, you could. But 's'different for me. Got a life to lead, you know, and—oh!"

The witch had gone. She had melted suddenly into the green without warning, gone as though against her will, banished by a spell of her own making.

"Oh—now I've gone and upset her," thought Lizzie. "Gone into one of her huffs. But 's'true—I can't be at her beck and call the whole time."

It did not even occur to her that perhaps it was the witch who was at her beck and call.

"You be careful!" Lizzie jumped at the voice out of thin air. "You—be—careful! I could *go—for ever*!"

7

"Come on, then." It was Gramma, and she kept walking. "Not all day to moon about in graveyards."

Thankfully, Lizzie followed, and once back in Kirk Street again she breathed a sigh of relief. She liked walking about Little Hemlock with Gramma, but it was usually more like a triumphal procession than a walk, punctuated by long chats, by stepping inside cottages for cups of tea, and waves left and right. Gramma had lived all her life in Little Hemlock up to six years ago when she had left to live near one of Patty's sisters who kept a little shop and needed help. Gramma knew everyone—even the handful of newcomers, whose histories she pieced together from second-hand snippets of information, so that by the time she actually did meet them they too seemed like old friends, and she would greet them as such, to their bafflement. Everyone Gramma met, she spoke to.

Today, Lizzie wanted Gramma to herself, which was why she had suggested walking along footpaths.

"Let's go up to't Braille wood, Gram," she said now. "Up through't allotments, over cow pastures and that."

Gramma nodded and went briskly on. Up the little jitty they went, and past the post office to the allotments, without meeting a single soul. Working on his allotment, was Jack Jackson. He did not see Lizzie and Gramma, and they stood there, staring.

"Where's it gone?" whispered Lizzie at last. "Footpath—it's gone!"

Gramma drew herself up.

"Jack!" she called. "Jack Jackson!"

He straightened up then, and turned.

"I'll have a word, if you please," said Gramma.

Jack Jackson, whom Gramma had known from childhood ("thievingest, slyest little brat in't village," she said) came now to her bidding. He advanced, at least, a few paces.

"Morning, Mrs Bailey," he said. "Grand day."

Gramma did not agree with him, and he coughed and

grew uncomfortable in the silence.

"Not matter even if we have a drop o' rain," he offered.
"All right for lettuces. They'll not want umbrellas."
He gave his humourless laugh.

"Lettuces," said Gramma grimly, "is neither here nor
there. Where's that footpath?"

"Aye. Well . . . you see, Mrs Bailey," he began.

"I do not see, Jack Jackson," interrupted Gramma.
"There's a footpath—" she gestured with her umbrella—
"*there*, as's been there since I was a little child. As 'as
been there, Jack Jackson, for hundreds of years.
Hundreds and hundreds and hundreds."

Jack Jackson, evidently dazzled by this unreeling of the
centuries, merely scratched his head and looked at
his lettuces.

"And *now*," went on Gramma, "it's gone to lettuces!"

"Aye. Well . . . you see, Mrs Bailey," began Jack
Jackson again, "there's no real *call* for footpaths, you see,
not these days. You got to *cultivate* land, see. Up the
yield. Hundreds lettuces up, I am, wi'out that path
cutting straight through."

"Listen you here," said Gramma. "It's no difference
if you're a thousand lettuces up. It's no difference if
you're a *million*. You get that path put back. And quick!"

Jack Jackson looked helplessly at her and then back at
his careful rows of vegetables and Lizzie could see that he
was wondering how you put a path back, quickly. Then
he seemed to rally, and straightened up and said with
something like a show of spirit,

"No '*arm* done, Mrs Bailey. No other complaints,
there's been. If you was wanting to get to't cow pastures,
you could always go't back way, see, up Tenter's Lane.
Else you could come up here, see," he indicated the path
that ran up the side of his garden, "and then get to't stile
along back, if you was careful not to tread on
my lettuces."

"I'll give you tread on your lettuces!" cried Gramma.
"*I* ain't going tramping through soil, not at my time of

9

life. And I know my rights, what's more. *Law* against
digging up footpaths, and the law's what I'll have on you,
Jack Jackson, if you don't get that path put back quick!"

"Aye, well," said Jack Jackson, "that's putting things
a bit strong. There's other paths gone from round here,
besides this, you know. You got to move wi' the times.
Progress."

"Don't you stand there telling me about progress!"
shrieked Gramma. She waved her umbrella then. "Don't
you go turning six pennorth o' lettuces into progress,
not in my hearing. And I'm warning you, Jack Jackson.
If that footpath ain't put back where it belongs by
tomorrow morning, there'll be steps taken."

Jack Jackson, speechless, stared. Even Lizzie could
not help wondering whether Gramma thought the path
had been rolled up, like a stair carpet, and could be put
down again as easily.

"Come along, Lizzie!" snapped Gramma, and off they
went, back the way they had come, the walk over.

"Drat Jack Jackson and his blessed lettuces," thought Lizzie. "That's our walk spoilt, thanks to him."

At dinner time Gramma held an inquest on the missing footpath.

"Don't know what you're making such a fuss about," said Patty. "Not end o't world."

"Aye, Patty," said Albert, "that's whole point. Folks don't make fusses, and footpaths go. There's dozens gone from round here, as *I* know about. *You* might not like walking, lass, but there's plenty do."

"My teacher says that," put in Lizzie eagerly. "Miss Platt—she says we've all to look after countryside. Nation's heritage, that's what she calls it."

"All *I* know is," said Patty, "that if folks like that Jack Jackson can make a bit extra by way of digging up footpaths, dig 'em up they will. That Jack Jackson'd dig up his own *grandmother* for lettuces."

"Against law, though, Patty," said Albert.

"Aye, well, that wouldn't bother him overmuch, either," returned Patty sourly.

"Means there's summat we can *do* about it, though, Patty," said Albert, quiet, but kindled too.

"Oooh, what, Dad?" cried Lizzie.

"Stamp on 'em," said Gramma briefly. "Stamp on his blessed lettuces. *I* will!"

"Not *stamp*, Gramma, not exact," Albert told her. "Summat more—planned, like. What they did at Mapleburn last year. What you do, see, is organise a proper walk, a walk on't footpaths, for everybody, like."

"Oooh—I remember!" Lizzie cried. "And they made it into a treasure hunt, wi' a picnic. Mary Bell went from our school, and she said it was smashing. Won second prize she did—a paperweight it was, all out of glass!"

"That's kind of thing, Lizzie," nodded Albert.

"And who's to organise it, pray?" demanded Patty. "As if I needed to ask."

"Wouldn't be that big a bother, Patt," said Albert apologetically. "Bit of an interest, in fact. Put clues in

rhymes we could, like they did at Mapleburn."

"Rhymes!" Patty laughed. "You?"

"Like—like for instance . . ." Albert cleared his throat:

    "Take the turning to the right
    And a stile will come into your sight."

They stared at him, every one of them, and it was Patty who broke the silence.

"You made that *up*?" she asked. "This *minute*?"

"Well. . . ." Albert cleared his throat again. "Aye."

"Well!" Patty was astonished. "I should never've known you'd got it in you. What was it again?"

    "Take the turning to the right
    And a stile will come into your sight."

Albert repeated it diffidently, trying to hide his pleasure in his unexpected success as poet.

"Well! If you can do it, Albert, you do it," cried Patty warmly then. "I never!"

"We could all help," put in Lizzie. "*I* can think of a rhyme as well:

    Run until your feet do tingle

And find a clue inside the Pingle!"

"Lovely!" cried Patty, clasping her hands.

And, "Aye, that'd do," agreed Albert. So the whole thing was settled. A footpath walk, which was to be a Village Treasure Hunt and Picnic would be organised for one Saturday afternoon. Only the Arbuckles themselves and Miss Platt, the schoolmistress, were to know the clues, and where the treasure lay.

"Oooh yes, Miss Platt'd help, all right," Lizzie told them. "On'y thing is, wi' me being in on it, shan't be able to win prize, shall I? What'll prize be, Dad?"

"Oh—summat," he replied. "Ask Miss Platt, you could—see what she thinks."

And so began a rhyming time for the Arbuckles. Rhymes went to their heads, they seemed to be rhyming even in their sleep. Even Patty was caught up in it. Lizzie found her one morning up to her elbows in suds, staring out the window and saying:

> "When you come to Cherry Tree
> On the gate a clue you'll see!"

over and over again, as if unable to believe in her own powers.

Miss Platt provided ten of the clues and promised to help lay the trail the night before. She also said that she would give the first prize. Gramma did not altogether approve of Miss Platt because she was against stamping on Jack Jackson's lettuces.

"What we must do," Miss Platt said, when Lizzie told her about the missing footpath, "is walk between them by all means, but as carefully as we can. Remember, Lizzie 'The purpose of war is peace'. You can disagree with a neighbour without there being any spite about it."

Gramma, when Lizzie repeated this precept to her later, was unimpressed. Lizzie felt sure that Gramma, who after all was no pupil of Miss Platt's, would stamp on Jack Jackson's lettuces willy-nilly. In fact, so far as Gramma was concerned, this was the sole purpose of the exercise.

Lizzie and Jonathan, now firm allies for the time being, made posters to put in the Post Office and on the notice board by the Memorial Hall. There was to be no charge for entering, and it soon became apparent that on the day fixed for the Treasure Hunt, almost the entire population of Little Hemlock would be tiptoeing through Jack Jackson's lettuces. Not, of course, that they knew this. As far as they were concerned, this was to be a Treasure Hunt and Picnic, and they all wanted to be there.

The night before the Treasure Hunt, Lizzie, who had spent the evening helping Miss Platt to lay the trail, was sure she would never be able to go to sleep. Patty came up as usual to turn off her light and tuck her in, and Lizzie asked her: "Are you excited, Mam?"

"Excited? Whatever about?"

"You know—treasure hunt, and that."

"Oh—that!" Patty pulled the blankets tight. "Take more'n that to excite me. And what you've to be excited about I don't know. You know all't clues, don't you?"

"Mmm. Helped Miss Platt put 'em down. Wrote 'em all in indelible ink she has, case o' rain."

"And that wouldn't surprise me," said Patty. "Now get off to sleep."

She kissed Lizzie, turned off the light, and went downstairs. Lizzie lay there, wide-eyed in the half dark.

"Won't rain," she murmured. "Lovely, it'll be . . . ooh, and picnic in't buttercup field. . . ."

She lay seeing pictures of bright acres, blinding gold with buttercups. She pictured herself roly-polying down the steep grass slopes of Hell Hills, and before long her pictures dissolved into dreams. She was asleep.

Lizzie was woken by the bell of her alarm clock, set for eight o'clock. She put out a hand automatically to turn it off, then lay there, luxuriously coming to.

"Oh—today," she thought, "it's today!"

Still she lay, and became aware then of a light rustling, a steady pattering, a—wide-awake in an instant, she scrambled down her bed and pulled aside the curtain.

"Oh no!"

The rain went rolling down the window in great pear-shaped drops and the view of the church and the green was blurred and misty. Lizzie stared for a few seconds then ran downstairs. The others were already up and drinking tea.

"Oh Mam, Dad—look at it! It'll ruin it!"

"Well, I did say," said Patty, as if her prediction of rain had in some mysterious way produced it.

"You take no notice," said Gramma. "Needed a drop o' rain, di'n't we, Albert?"

"But the Treasure Hunt!"

"Rain before seven, fine before eleven," said Gramma, unperturbed.

"Oh—you never believe that!" Patty was scornful.

"If you'd lived as long as *I* have, my lass," said Gramma, "*you'd* believe it."

Patty, who had *not* lived as long as Gramma, said

no more.

"Could only be a shower, Lizzie," said Albert. "Early yet. *Do* wi' a spot o' rain, like Gramma says. Ground's fair cracking wi' dryness. And hunt don't even start till two. Can't rain till then."

"Rain before seven, fine before eleven," repeated Gramma maddeningly, and Lizzie went to the window and stared out, and thought: "*Could* rain all day—'course it could. Forty days and forty nights, it could, if it felt like it...!"

Lizzie could see the church tower from where she stood, and seeing it she thought of the graveyard, and then—the witch.

"What if... I wonder if... no.... Worth trying, though. If 't'hasn't stopped raining by... by half-past ten, I'll go. No harm...."

It had not stopped raining by half-past ten, and Lizzie accordingly put on her anorak and went out. Toby, in sou'wester and oilskins, was making mud pies. Lizzie edged past him and went up Church Lane and over Kirk

Street and into the churchyard. When she went through the iron gate she hesitated a little. The graveyard was dank and dripping. It was full of unaccustomed stir and sound, and yet, curiously, more empty and alone than it had ever seemed under the sun.

Lizzie had not for one moment imagined that the witch would be sitting, intrepid, on the tomb of the Perfectly Peaceful Posts knitting her wet wool, oblivious of the steadily falling rain. She was not even certain that the witch would materialise in the rain even if Lizzie called her.

"After all," she thought, "if she comes visible, she'll get wet. "'Spect she's dry, *invisible*."

She thought of something else, too. Lately, the witch had become less and less predictable. Often she would not appear at all, and even on the days when she did, would hardly have a word for Lizzie. She just sat there, counting stitches under her breath and sulking.

"Witch!" called Lizzie, and the word seemed to hang forlornly for an instant in the drift of rain. She called again: "Witch! It's me—Lizzie!"

She felt ridiculous, standing there wet and alone, talking to herself, it seemed.

"No good," she thought. "Might've known."

She turned and walked slowly back past the dripping laurels by the side of the church, and as she did so heard the witch's voice, mirthful and infuriating: "Rain before seven, fine before eleven!"

Lizzie whirled about. "Witch?"

She paused only an instant before going on again. She was not in the mood for games of hide and seek. Just as she put her hand on the wet, cold metal of the little gate, she heard it again: "Rain before seven, fine before eleven!" and a long, fading cackle of laughter.

Lizzie marched on. As she passed the Memorial Hall she looked up at the poster she and Jonathan had made and saw that the colours were beginning to run. She crossed the road, and as she did so the church clock

began to strike eleven. Head down, she kicked a stone all the way home and stamped in puddles. She went past Toby, muddy and red-cheeked in the border, and into the living-room where Patty was cutting bread.

"There you are!" cried Gramma triumphantly. "What did I tell you!"

"What?" Lizzie was tugging at her wellingtons.

"Rain before seven, fine before eleven!"

"But—but it hasn't, it—"

Lizzie, right by the door still, threw it open.

"It has!"

And she had not even noticed, eyes glued on the ground, kicking stones through puddles.

"Hurray!" she shouted. "And sun's coming through—'t'is—see it, behind't church!"

At two o'clock Lizzie was by the milk table by Stokes's farm, which was the starting point, helping Miss Platt give out cards. There was one between each family, and each party was sent off at two-minute intervals. Gram took a card.

"Don't know half clues," she said. "*Heard* 'em enough times, but not to know 'em."

Lizzie pulled at Albert's sleeve.

"Eeeeh—look! Mam, look! It's them!"

Coming up Main Street laden with carrier bags and unmistakably headed for the Treasure Hunt, were Jack Jackson and family.

"Oh my good gracious!" exclaimed Patty.

"Steady on, pair on you," said Albert evenly. "Nowt amiss in that. Afternoon, Jack. Afternoon Irma. And how's Steven? Going to win't Treasure Hunt, are you?"

"Aye," said Steven eagerly. "Dad and Mam've won a hunt before, on'y in a car. Dad's laid me five to one we'll win!"

"Aye, well—you've won then, young 'un, whatever happens," said Albert. "Covered both ways, as they say."

"It's to be hoped grass ain't still damp, for't picnic," said Irma. "Not really my cup o' tea, picnics. But there you are. They would come."

"Here we are, then, Mr Jackson," said Miss Platt. "This is yours. You'll notice you have to collect various items as you go along, before you give in the card at the end."

Then the Jackson family were off at a fast walk to follow the first clue and to walk, eventually, through their own lettuces.

"Can *we* go next, Miss Platt," cried Lizzie. "I could go along wi' Gram—I'd not help her, honest, and we'd not take prize even if we won it. Dad and Mam're going straight there, to take Toby, but I'd like to go on't trail!"

"Very well, Lizzie," said Miss Platt. "I can manage now, thank you."

Lizzie and Gramma set off.

"Let's miss first three clues out," said Lizzie, once they were out of earshot. "Then we could take short cut up

jitty and see his face when he gets to his lettuces."

"No, I shan't do that," said Gramma righteously. "Matter of *principle* this is, Lizzie, and no need for any o' that."

"Well *I* shall," thought Lizzie rebelliously. "I shall hide behind't hedge and *watch* 'em."

And so she did. By the time Jack Jackson reached the lettuce patch Gramma was away over the field towards Pulpit Ash, a lone black figure on the green, and a public footpath was already beginning to take shape again among the lettuces. (Gramma, true to her word, had stamped on several, and Lizzie, close behind, had followed suit.)

The Jacksons came to a halt and Lizzie could see a scowl on Jack's face, a considerable one, even from that distance.

"Oooh, Jack, your lettuces!" She heard Irma's scream. "Oooh—I told you not to do that, I did, and now look!"

"I see," said Jack ominously, once he had taken things

in. "Come on now, quick—fast, pair on you! Win this I will now, or bust!" and the Jacksons came steaming through their own lettuces so fast that Lizzie barely had time to creep round the hedge out of their sight.

Lizzie ran a different way then to rejoin Gramma by Pulpit Ash. After that, Gramma gave up the hunt too, and she and Lizzie took another short cut, to Hell Hills where the picnic was to be. Albert and Patty and several others were already there. Toby was roly-polying on the slope with squeals of delight. Lizzie ran to him and gave him little pushes till faster and faster he went, tumbling right to the very bottom, a chuckling, red-faced bundle.

"Oooh, smashing . . ." Lizzie lay on her back and sniffed the smell of clover made strong by rain with hot sun following. Jonathan came whirling down too, and after a while they went back up and rolled down again, racing.

"Smashing old hill, this," Lizzie told him. "Should see us sledding down it, in winter. Hey, does your Aunt Blodwen *let* you roll down hills?" Jonathan tore up handfuls of grass and flowers and pelted Lizzie with them, and she ducked away, squealing.

The food came next. The Arbuckles had sausage rolls, ham and egg sandwiches, chocolate cake and apples— and almost anything else you could think of, because what Lizzie didn't have she could always swap for with someone else.

Then Miss Platt stood up to announce the winners.

"First prize goes to the one who followed the trail correctly," she said, "brought all the items asked for, and lastly, found five different kinds of wild flower here on Hell Hills. And that prize," she paused, "goes to— Jack Jackson and family!"

"Well dang me!" cried Gramma, regardless of the Jacksons who were sitting only a few yards away. The people of Little Hemlock, who knew a joke when they saw one, cheered and yelled as Jack went up to take his prize. Each and every one of them had trampled through

Jack Jackson's lettuce patch, so it was really a kind of poetic justice.

Jack took his prize, a long cardboard roll, and started back to his place.

"What's in it, Lizzie?" whispered Patty, and Lizzie shook her head.

"Don't know, Mam. Miss Platt gave it."

"Well fair does," said Albert, and clapped with the rest. As Jack came back to his place he shot a triumphant look towards the Arbuckles.

"Well done, Jack," said Albert. "What've you got there, then?"

"Yes, go on, Jack, open it up," cried Irma fussily. "My word, fancy our winning!"

"Aye, fancy!" Lizzie heard Gramma mutter, and turned aside her own face to hide a smile. Jack put his fingers in the end of the roll and drew out a paper.

"A picture!" cried Irma. "That's what it is!"

Jack unrolled it and stared blankly for a moment. Albert went round behind and looked over his shoulder.

"Map!" said Jack at last.

"Aye," said Albert, straight faced, "be a lot o' use will that, Jack. Ordinance Survey, large scale, see, o' Little Hemlock. Every last field, hedge, ditch and footpath on there."

And Albert winked, very deliberately, at Lizzie and Gramma, and Jack, over the top of his map, glared at the innocent Arbuckles and Lizzie thought, "Oooh—we won, after all!"

And she did not wait even to hear the other prizes, she threw herself into another mad roly-poly. The grass, the shouting, the clover and the sky whirled together in her head and she thought, "Oooh, what a perfect day!" and could hardly contain her happiness. Because perfect days, as Lizzie well knew, don't grow on trees.

Lizzie Dripping

by the Sea

"Oooh Dad!" squealed Lizzie Dripping. "Smashing!"

"What, just like that?" cried Patty. "Up and off wi'out a minute's notice?"

"I reckon that's way to do it," said Albert. "Run up on it while it ain't looking, like. Ages since we last had sniff o't sea."

"Cough cough cough all winter, I was," Gramma said, and coughed hard now to illustrate it. "Need a sniff o' sea, I do."

"Well, I've eggs, o' course," said Patty dubiously, taking mental stock of her larder. "And I can always open a tin o' salmon, and there's—"

"Look, Patty luv," said Albert, "give over, will you? We shall go to a cafe."

"A cafe?" cried Patty. "Just hark at him! But price, Albert!"

"You never mind about price. We shall get up at six, set off for Yarbury and have us dinners at a cafe—one of them along sea front."

'Oooh, it would be nice," said Patty. "Always put in a few hard-boiled eggs, and that, to fill us."

"Can Jonathan go?" asked Lizzie then. "Told him I'd play tomorrow. And he'd like it."

"So long as that scrubby little aunt of his don't come," put in Gramma.

Patty and Albert exchanged looks.

"She'll have to be *asked*, Ma," said Patty. "And she is my friend, you know."

"She'll not go," put in Lizzie. "Not tidy enough, seaside ain't, not for her."

"And that'll do from you, miss," said Patty.

"Don't see how she can go, anyhow," Lizzie muttered. "There'll be no room, not for all them people."

"Aye, well, you see," said Albert. "I've fixed up wi' Bill Larkin to borrow his car. Swap, like, for't day."

"Oooh, we have got things off pat, haven't we," cried Patty, excited again. "You nip off down to Blodwen's now, Lizzie, and see if they'll come. Six o'clock, tell 'em, and we'll pick 'em up."

Lizzie was through the door in a moment and heard Patty's voice after her : "And not to bother wi' sandwiches, tell her. Tell her we shall go to a cafe."

"Wheee !" Lizzie sped down the garden path and could smell, even in the midst of her excitement, the strong night smell of lavender and stock and drying grass. There in the road, in place of Albert's old van, was

Bill Larkin's estate car, big and shining.

"Oooh—'s'all true, then!" and Lizzie pelted on.

At the corner of Church Lane, on an impulse, she ran straight over the road and up along the side of the church and took the short cut into the graveyard. She stood panting long enough to see that the witch was not there disguised as a black shadow in the low evening sunlight. Then she cupped her hands to her mouth and yelled, "Not coming tomorrer, witch! Sorry—can't. Going to't seaside! Yippee! Tara, witch!"

And giving the witch not the blink of an eye in which to reply she was off again, through the rich gold of the evening, to tell the news to Aunt Blodwen and Jonathan.

Lizzie was awake at dawn when the birds were whistling and a faint milky haze over the hills of Mapleburn promised a day of glorious heat. The Arbuckles packed their belongings into the car and set off.

"You'd think we was going for a week, all this stuff!" cried Patty. She settled luxuriously into her seat beside Albert. "Oooh, lovely car this is, feel like a queen, don't you?"

"Get yourself killed in any car," said Gramma. "And a little 'un'll do it as good as a big 'un.''

"Ehy up, Albert," cried Patty, "right, here, remember. Blodwen yet."

"And my luck to get sat next to her," said Gramma sourly. She peered out the window as Albert drew up outside Blodwen's trim little house. Lizzie saw the net curtains at the window twitch and next minute Aunt Blodwen came out, with Jonathan following.

"Well!" exclaimed Gramma. "Dolled up like the dog's dinner! Just you look at that! Reckons she's going to Buckingham Palace, that one does!"

"Sssh, Ma!" hissed Patty.

"And look at him!" cried Lizzie. "Oh Mam, she'll never let him play on beach!"

"Sssh!" hissed Patty again, and wound down her

window.

"Next Gramma, Blodwen," she said. "And Jonathan in't back wi' Lizzie and Toby."

Gramma shuffled ungraciously across the back seat so that she was sitting at the extreme far side, right against the door.

"My word," said Aunt Blodwen as Albert drove off. "Posh we are, today. Lovely car, Albert."

She snuggled fussily into her corner and Lizzie in the back made faces at Jonathan and pointed at his clothes and he in turn made faces at Aunt Blodwen's back and pointed at *her*.

"Lovely day, by the look of it," went on Aunt Blodwen. "It's to be hoped Yarbury won't be full of day trippers. Lowers the tone of a place, day trippers, I always think."

Gramma, a mint imperial poised at her lips, spoke up then from her corner. "*We're* only going for't day," she said.

"Oh!" Aunt Blodwen gave a light little laugh.

"Not like *us* for heaven's sake! *Real* day trippers, that's what I meant, see—eating chips out of paper bags and kids screaming . . . snagging your tights wi' their buckets and spades!"

She shuddered, and no one spoke for a moment. Then Albert struck up, "I do like to be beside the seaside!"

"I do like to be beside the sea . . ." chorused Patty and Lizzie.

And after that they rollicked along as all the best day trippers do, while Aunt Blodwen pursed her lips and smoothed her skirts and made it perfectly plain that she was wishing, already, that she had never come.

By nine o'clock the Arbuckles were at Yarbury and the first things they saw were big posters, and banners hung across the streets. As soon as Albert drew the car up in the park on the front Lizzie got out and ran over to read one of the posters.

"Yarbury Carnival Week, June the third to the tenth. Oooh, that's today!" she cried. "It's seventh today, and look, Mam, fancy dress parade at two-thirty! Oh—I wish I'd known—could've dressed up!"

"Pity we didn't check before we started," said Aunt Blodwen. "Day trippers galore, I shouldn't wonder."

"Get down to beach, shall we?" suggested Albert.

"Oooh yes!" cried Lizzie. And the moment she saw the sea her legs seemed to go wild with excitement of their own accord, and she jumped off the promenade onto the sand and ran in wide, giddy circles, laughing and shrieking. At last she collapsed, dizzy and breathless, and lay with her eyes shut and listened to the gulls and the falling waves and thought for a moment that she actually felt the world stop turning, and time standing still. She put out her hand and felt the cool sand trickle between her fingers and thought,

"I can hear't sea, right through't sand. . . . I feel like a sea shell. Wouldn't mind being a sea shell . . . one o' them curly ones. . . ."

28

She sat up there and looked about for the others. They were still standing where she had left them, and it looked as if they were having an argument.

"Aunt Blodwen, I s'pose," she thought, and got up. "Spoil everything, she will." And she climbed up again and joined them.

"Well, you know best, Blodwen," Patty was saying, in a voice that said the exact opposite. "If it's shops you've come to see, you go and *look* at shops."

"No harm *Jonathan* going on beach," said Aunt Blodwen, "so long as he behaves hisself and keeps hisself clean."

Lizzie said the last words to herself, in chorus with Aunt Blodwen.

"See you in cafe then, shall we?" said Albert. "Lobster Pot at one o' clock."

"And you behave yourself, Jonathan," said Aunt Blodwen, "an' do as you're told, and mind you keep yourself clean."

Again Lizzie mouthed the words in unison and she pulled a face after Aunt Blodwen's retreating back.

"Good riddance," she whispered to Jonathan, and he nodded.

"That's her out way, then," remarked Gramma cheerfully. "On beach shall we, Albert? Get us deckchairs put up?"

The Arbuckles accordingly staked their claim on Yarbury beach. A windbreak was put up, after a great deal of argument as to which way the wind was blowing, and Toby was given a bucket and spade.

("That'll settle him, for't morning," observed Patty.) Gramma took out her knitting.

"Oh, Gram!" cried Lizzie. "You're never going to knit!"

"And why not?" enquired Gramma. "Not one for idling, me, seaside or no."

"But you can knit at home!" Lizzie persisted. "Come and paddle—go on, Gram, do!"

"I never in this world shall!" retorted Gramma. "Legs like I've got, and paddle?"

"You will, Mam, won't you," pleaded Lizzie.

"And Dad?"

"Have a bit of a dabble later, I might," said Albert. "You and Jonathan run down, eh, and let me know what water's like?"

He had rolled up his shirt sleeves and his trouser legs, and now sat back in his deckchair and began to light his pipe.

"Dratted pattern," muttered Gramma. "Which way's out? Can't tell which from which...!"

"Witch from witch..." Lizzie caught the words and translated them.

"Witch..." she thought. "Funny... can't hardly believe in her, not here... Wonder if she heard what I said last night. Wonder if she's waiting...?"

And no sooner had the thought dissolved than she thought she saw, for the merest fraction of a minute, a raggedy black shape away on the tideline, a pointed hat. Lizzie gasped, shut her eyes and shook her head hard to settle her brains.

"Oooh look!" shrieked Patty, and Lizzie, startled, jerked up, her eyes wide open again.

"By heck!" said Gramma. "A bear!"

"And a witch!" cried Patty. "Look, Lizzie! Look, Toby—bear!"

"Bear!" repeated Toby, wide-eyed.

Lizzie, very slowly, turned her head, prepared for the worst.

Strolling along Yarbury sands arm in arm were, indeed, a bear and a witch. Lizzie shut her eyes again quickly.

"Oh—what's she doing?" she thought desperately. "Oooh—she's *follered* me! What'll I *do*?"

"Here Albert!" She heard Patty's voice. "Get camera—look sharp!"

Lizzie opened her eyes again. The witch was right near-by now.

"*Not* her!" She actually said the words out loud, so enormous, so overwhelming was her relief.

"You what? said Patty absently. "Come on, Albert, you'll miss 'em!"

"Don't look owt like a witch!" thought Lizzie scornfully. "Proper fancy dress witch she is—don't she *know* what a real witch looks like?"

The witch in question was about ten years old. She wore a false nose on a band of elastic, had fair hair tangled among the grey wool that sprouted from under her hat, and brown sandals and white socks were clearly visible beneath her cloak. Also, her eyes were blue.

"Take a picture, can I?" asked Albert.

"All right!" came a high, unwitchlike voice. A hand came out from under the cloak and poked the bear in the middle. "Stand *still* Mark, will you, the man wants to

take our pictures."

The bear and the witch both stood stiffly to attention and Albert clicked the camera.

"Ta!" he said. "In for t'fancy dress, are you?"

The bear nodded.

"'S'hot in here," came a muffled voice.

"Aye, well, have to take your head off and cool down," said Albert. "Have to take your head off for your dinner anyhow, shan't you?"

The bear nodded again.

"'S'all right him talking," said the witch. "My *nose* hurts. I *told* Mam it'd hurt."

"Best take nose off then, an' all," suggested Albert. "Not till 's'afternoon is it, parade?"

"Here, look," said the witch, pulling at the bear's slack fur, "there's that stupid Susan Coombes coming, all got up in a sheet! Come on, Mark, quick, afore she sees us!"

The bear and the witch moved smartly off and the Arbuckles turned to see three other apparitions strolling towards them.

"Don't it seem queer, though?" cried Patty. "Never seen sights like *this* on't beach afore. Ghost, look—and what's she. . . ?"

Lizzie did not hear the rest, because all of a sudden it seemed that the gulls were shrieking and flying in storm as if panicked. And mingled with their cries she thought she heard the coarse, unmistakable cackle of a witch, so she looked back towards the sea and saw, quite distinctly, the witch again, on the tideline, like some impossible flotsam.

"Let's go and paddle!" she heard Jonathan say. "Come on, Lizzie!"

She thought rapidly.

"I know!" she cried "You go that way!" and she pointed wildly, away from the witch. "And I'll go t'other, and first—first to find a crab shell buys t'other an ice lolly!"

"Right!" said Jonathan. "First back here with a crab shell!" and he was off, spurting sand.

"That's him out way," thought Lizzie. "Now. . . ."

And she began to walk steadily towards the witch, keeping her eyes fixed on her.

"One thing," she thought, "won't matter if they *do* see her, not here. Think she's a fancy dress witch, they will. . . ."

"Hee hee!" She heard the witch's cackle, oddly camouflaged today because of the squarking of the gulls.

The witch was paddling, skirts held up, more impossible now than she had ever seemed in Little Hemlock, among the gravestones. Lizzie stopped and stared at her.

"Hee!" cried the witch. "I like it, I do! Better'n knitting! Hee!"

"But you shouldn't've come!" cried Lizzie. "You shouldn't've!"

The witch turned on her, her eyes flashing green
sparks.

"And why not?" she snapped. "Anywhere you go,
I can go, girl, remember that! Anywhere!"

"Oh I know—I know that," said poor Lizzie. "But
what if—what if Mam and Dad was to see you,
or Jonathan?"

The witch cackled merrily and did not answer. She
kicked her skinny feet in the water and made herself a
halo of spray.

"Lucky for you there's a fancy dress," said Lizzie.
"Lucky for me, an' all. One thing, anyhow. Don't
believe in witches, Jonathan don't. Told me so."

"Don't—*what*?"

The witch advanced out of the sea and was all at once menacing again, a witch-on-holiday changed to a witch-on-business in the blink of an eye.

"*Everyone* don't, you know!" said Lizzie desperately. "'S'not just him!"

"Hmmmm..."

The witch was looking past Lizzie at something beyond, and turning, Lizzie saw Jonathan approaching, holding something aloft on the end of a stick.

"Got one!" she heard his faint cry. "I've won!"

"Not toads...." the witch was murmuring, "don't fit, toads at sea. Crab! That's it! Turn crab...."

"Oh, you—oh, not him!" cried Lizzie aghast. "He's got an Auntie Blodwen, and she'd kill me!"

But the witch was already raising her skinny hands and Jonathan was coming nearer every moment, blissfully unaware that crabhood was only a pincer's breadth away.

"Now!" cried the witch.

Lizzie shut her eyes. She heard the scream of gulls, the crash of waves, and Jonathan's voice, oddly blurred and far away: "Lizzie! Come on—what's up?"

Lizzie opened her eyes and was looking down at the wet sand strewn with weeds and stones. There, right by her foot, was a large crab—a live crab.

She screamed then. She screamed loudly and madly and felt herself being shaken and looked up to see Jonathan's face only a few inches off her own and screamed again, one last scream.

"S'only a crab!" he cried.

"I thought—I thought—" stammered Lizzie. She looked down. The crab was still there. She looked at where the witch was and saw that the witch was not, and wondered fleetingly whether it was *herself* she had changed into a crab.

"Trust a girl to be afraid of a crab," said Jonathan, and began to walk off. "Anyhow, we didn't say a live crab, so I've still won, and I'll have an orange wopper, thanks."

Lizzie glared after him, then followed.

"Orange wopper's what you'd've been," she thought, "if she'd've done that spell, and you ended up on a slab ..."

"Well!" said Patty as they stepped outside again into the cold, sea-smelling air. "That was a yarking good meal, Albert, whatever *she* says!" (With a jerk of the head towards Gramma.) "I'm that full I can hardly stir."

"I don't say owt about food," said Gramma. "Food was all right. What I'm saying is, I can't abide my dinner off a pink plate. For cakes, pink plates is, and don't go with roast and greens at all. Particular carrots. Nasty, carrots is, off pink plates."

"Oh shush up, Ma, do, about pink plates!" cried Patty. "Now what about this here fancy dress? Watch that, shall us, while our dinners go down?"

"Not me, Patty, if you don't mind," said Blodwen.

"Go to't Bingo shall you, then? asked Patty.

"Oh!" Aunt Blodwen gave her light, superior Welsh laugh. "No, thank you, Patty."

"I shall go down Bingo later on," announced Gramma. She popped in a mint imperial, and poked her tongue about among her teeth. "I could do wi' some new teeth, you know."

Blodwen shuddered delicately.

"Meet you at car park shall I then?" she said. "Six o' clock, is it?"

"We shan't go wi'out you, Blodwen," said Albert.

"More's pity!" thought Lizzie.

But Blodwen out of sight was quickly forgotten, and by the time the Arbuckles had stationed themselves on the beach the fancy dress parade was about to begin.

"There's that bear!" cried Jonathan. "Look, Mr Arbuckle, one you took picture of!"

"And there's witch!" cried Patty.

Lizzie looked and saw the bear and the witch. Behind them she saw something else.

"Oh no!" she cried inwardly.

Walking behind Humpty Dumpty and in front of Little Bo Peep was the witch. She was smiling happily and making exaggerated bows and waves on either hand, as if all the applause in Yarbury were meant for her alone.

"One thing," thought Lizzie, "she'll not win. Can't. There's two witches, and they can't both win prize!"

She looked sideways at the faces of those nearest to her for signs that they had realised that this was a real witch they were looking at, but they were cheering and clapping and pointing and taking photographs in the most ordinary way possible. You might almost have thought they did not see the witch at all, Lizzie thought, so obvious did it seem to her that this was no fancy dress witch, but a real, live, spelling, toad-turning witch, who lived in a graveyard and could turn the world upside down if she wanted.

The witch looked straight into Lizzie's eyes then and grinned wickedly. Lizzie shook her head and frowned, but the witch stretched up a thin hand, snapped her fingers, and a bunch of balloons was all at once there, like bubbles bursting into the air. Lizzie gasped. Now, surely, someone would point a finger and shout,

"Look out! A witch! Beware!"

But no one did, and the witch went by and out of sight and by the time Lizzie had collected herself a voice was coming over the loudspeakers.

"Fancy dress competitors will now assemble on foot in front of the judges for the final line-up. Our judges will be Alderman J. Cornforth, Mayor of Yarbury, and a visitor to the town, selected at random only a few minutes ago on the promenade. Would you mind telling us your name, madam?"

"Cole," came a familiar voice. "Mrs Blodwen Cole, from Little Hemlock."

"Ooooh!" shrieked Patty.

"Well I'll go to the foot of our stairs!" ejaculated Albert, removing his pipe from his mouth for the purpose.

"Her?" cried Gramma. "Judge?"

"Mrs Blodwen Cole has sportingly agreed to come along here and help our Mayor to decide on the winners," came the voice, "so shall we all give her a round of applause?"

"*I* ain't clapping," said Gramma disgustedly. "*I'd've* done it if I'd 'a' known they was a judge short."

"There'll be no holding her now," said Patty.

The fancy dress competitors were walking round in a circle now beneath the promenade where the judges sat. The witch was still there. She was simply standing in the middle while the others walked round her, as if she were playing "Poor Mary sat a-weeping."

"Oooh, what's she doing?" thought Lizzie desperately. "She thinks she's won! Oooh, what'll she do when she finds she ain't? Doing this to spite me, she is."

There was a renewed burst of applause and Lizzie saw that the Mayor was on his feet now, paper in hand, while Aunt Blodwen sat smirking beside him.

"Ladies and Gentlemen," he said, "—and children, of course—I and my charming co-judge," he bowed towards Aunt Blodwen who smirked the more and wriggled in her seat, "have unanimously decided on the winners. And first prize," he paused, "first prize goes to—the snail!"

A snail was pushed forward by the rest and moved up to the judge at a very un-snail-like pace. The judge wanted to shake hands and give the prize, but both the snail's hands were under its shell, so it stood there, quite helplessly, shaking its horns while the crowd laughed and cheered.

But what Lizzie saw was the witch's face, scowling and vengeful and her hands lifted, poised for spelling.

"Oooh—can't they see she's real?" thought Lizzie. "She'll have 'em all into seagulls! Ooh, let 'er have second prize, let her!"

But the judge was already announcing the second prize, and a Welsh lady with a conical witch's hat came mincing forward. Aunt Blodwen preened, the witch drew herself into a taut hunch of fury. A swift shake of the fist and a poisonous darting look at Aunt Blodwen and—she was gone!

Lizzie let out her breath.

"Thank goodness! But oh dear, she'll not've gone for good. Get her own back, that witch will, afore she's done. What'll she *do*, though . . . ? *Summat* awful. . . ."

"Giddy you get, doing this . . ." Lizzie stood ankle-deep and watched the water rushing up and then ebbing back, brown with a soft draining of sand and shingle and a pulling and falling away of the sand beneath her feet.

"Wish I lived at the sea . . . might do, when I grow up. Have one of them little kiosk things, up't pier. . . ."

She looked towards the pier. There was the witch, leaning on the white rails.

"Oh!" Lizzie's hand flew up to her mouth. The witch melted into air and became in the instant twice as alarming.

"Now where's she gone? Hanging over't place like a—like a blessed vulture! Trying to pay me out, I s'pose, for not going to't graveyard. But I *can't* every day—told her that afore. She should never've made me promise!"

The seagulls screeched noisily close at hand and Lizzie jumped nervously and watched them, almost expecting to see the witch in flight among them. And she could hear a voice in the clamour: "Them that breaks a promise, pays a forfeit!"

Lizzie turned her back on pier and gulls alike, and paddled back along the creaming frill of the tide, savouring the cold salt on her feet and in her nostrils, but still, despite it all, she could not forget that witch.

"Funny thing is, how did she get here? How did she know where I was—never *told* her?"

A few waves later the thought occurred, "To do wi' *me*, that witch is. I thought she was to do wi't graveyard, mainly. But 's'not. 'S'me. . . ."

She pondered the matter for the break of another wave or two.

"Does anyone else see her, besides me? Anyone else in't whole world . . . ? Is she *my* witch, *really* mine . . . ? Ask others. . . ."

So she left the sea and went back to the rest of the Arbuckles who were burying Albert. He lay there like an effigy with a live flesh face. Even his face was whiskered with sand, and so comical that Lizzie forgot her question and found herself laughing and kneeling with the others to scoop sand over him.

"Steady!" said Albert. "Live to tell't tale, I should like to."

"If we covered your face now," said Jonathan, "you'd be dead. Dead and buried."

"Oh charming!" cried Patty. "Hear that, Albert?"

"Didn't say I would," said Jonathan. "But if I did, he would."

"*And* no joke," put in Gramma. "At seaside and talking about dead! Be quiet about dead, will you! And keep yourself clean, my lad, if you don't want that aunt of yours round your backside."

Albert raised himself up onto his elbows then and the sand crumpled and fell away and the game was over.

"Mam," said Lizzie, remembering, "did you see that witch?"

"Witch?" Patty was peeling a banana and only half listening.

"There was a witch with that bear," said Jonathan. "Your dad took a picture."

"Another witch, I mean," persisted Lizzie.

"Swarming wi' 'em, this place is," said Patty. "Bears, witches, frogs—never seen the like. That one"— (with a jerk of the head towards Toby) "—'ll about grow *up* thinking there's bears and frogs at seaside!"

41

"But a real one—*looking* real, I mean. Not fancy dress."

"Oh yes!" said Patty, sarcastic now. "In sky, you mean, on a broomstick?"

"Or invisible," suggested Jonathan innocently. "I saw an *invisible* witch."

Lizzie gritted her teeth hard.

"I just wish," she thought, "I'd *let* her turn you into a crab now. I wish you'd been made crab, boiled, and we'd all *ate* you, in sandwiches, wi' cress!"

"Tide's coming up fast," said Albert, who specialised in changing the subject if the occasion seemed to demand it. "Best start moving things up."

"Oooh!" cried Patty. "It *has* come up in a rush! Come along Lizzie, help get these things together, will you. And you'd best budge fast, Ma, if you don't want to get swep' out to sea."

Gramma did not budge.

"*That* one'll get swep' out to sea," she remarked, nodding. The Arbuckles all turned. The sea had swept in to fill a low wide dip and had left a spit of sand beyond still uncovered. On it was a solitary figure in a deckchair, facing out to sea, oblivious of the fact that she was already marooned.

"By heck!" said Albert. "*She'll* get her feet wet. Best give her a shout. Fallen off to sleep, likely, and not noticed."

He went forward, followed by the others, cupping his hands as he went and shouting: "Ahoy! Look out! Tide's coming! Ahoy!"

At the same time the deckchair boy came scooting down the beach in a spurt of sand, yelling and waving. "My chair that is!" he cried. "Corporation chair she's sitting on!"

He went splashing straight into the water and waded over, up to his knees. As he approached the figure in the deckchair rose and turned and let out a shrill scream. Albert and the others stood transfixed.

"It's Blodwen!" squealed Patty. "Oh—she'll be

drownded!"

"Help!" screamed Blodwen and lurched to the water's edge where she stood helplessly. The deckchair boy, ignoring her, grabbed up the chair and made back with it, splashing in again and sending a shower of spray right over Aunt Blodwen making her look, for a second, almost romantic.

"You want to watch it, missis!" they heard his voice. "Paid for this, I should've had to, out my wages, if you'd been swept off!"

Back he threshed, deckchair in tow. Aunt Blodwen bent and began to tear off her shoes and stockings and Lizzie, hand over her mouth now to hide the laughter that came irresistibly surging up, thought: "The witch! 'S'her doing, all right! Witch's revenge!"

"And mind you keep yourself clean!" she heard Jonathan splutter behind her. They all stood and watched while Aunt Blodwen, shoes and stockings held aloft, hat awry and water up above her skirts now, waded for safety.

"She *will* create!" Patty said.

"Her *turn* to get wet, I reckon," observed Gramma calmly behind them, and Blodwen moaned and squealed and lurched and all at once the day was made perfect— absolutely and beautifully, poetically perfect.

Lizzie Dripping

Says Goodbye

"Growing up now, you are, our Lizzie," Patty said. "Though sometimes I wonder if you ever will. And time you come down to earth a bit, never mind always off mooning about in graveyards."

"Not always," said Lizzie sulkily. "What's it to do wi' old Ma Bates, anyhow?"

"Nowt at all to do," said Gramma with asperity. "Wants to mind her own business, that one does. Not keeper o't graveyard, she's not, for owt I know."

"Not the point, Ma," said Patty. "Just mentioned it to me, that's all. *See* graveyard, she can, from her house."

"And good job she never saw *witch*," Lizzie thought.

"Not nice, anyhow," Patty went on. "Going off to play in graveyards. Concentrated ground that is, Lizzie. Show some respect for't dead, you're meant to, in them sort o' places."

"Dead'll not mind," observed Gramma with conviction. "Ma Bates as minds, not dead."

"Anyhow, you keep off from there, Lizzie," Patty said. "D'you hear? Plenty of other places to play, besides graveyards."

"I don't play, Mam," Lizzie told her. "I—I think and that."

"Oh! Think, is it?" cried Patty. "Nice cheerful thoughts you'll get there, I'll be bound! Downright morbid it is, a girl of your age. I don't know where you get it from, I don't really."

Lizzie said nothing.

"And what're you going to do wi' yourself today?"
Patty asked. "Because if you—"

"Project," said Lizzie quickly. "Holiday project."

"Oooh. Never had them sorts o' thing in my day,"
said Patty. "Not that I'm grumbling, mind. Keeps you
out road, anyhow. What is it you're doing this time,
then?"

"Oooh, it's ever so good! Miss Platt's idea it was.
What we're doing, see, is making a record of Little
Hemlock, for posterity."

"Posterity!" Patty threw up her hands. "Lawks—
whatever next!"

"We're doing everything about what it's like to be
alive in 1975, see," explained Lizzie. "Then it's to be put
in a tin box, and locked, and given parson to keep wi'
parish records, Miss Platt says. And on it it'll say
Not to be opened till 2075. We'll all be dead then. Even
I'll be dead, let alone you."

"Charming," said Patty. "Here we go again. Back to't graveyard. I begin to think you'll not be happy till you're buried."

"Then posterity'll know what it was like now, see," said Lizzie. "Posterity's the opposite of ancestors, you know. It means people who live *after* you."

"What sort o' things you putting in?" enquired Gramma. "You putting in price o' things? You want to put price o' things, Lizzie. That'll give 'em summat to think about. You put price of eggs—*and* a loaf! By heck, *that'll* give 'em summat to think about!"

"We ain't just doing things like that, Gram," Lizzie told her. "Though we are doing it, and putting in things like newspapers, and that—*Radio Times*. But we're doing about people as well, see. All got five each to interview, like. And we're to do our own families, and all. And Miss Platt said grandparents were very important. To ask them specially, she said."

"Did she, now," said Gramma, pleased, and shot Patty a triumphant look.

"Yes. 'Cos they can remember further back, see. So when they open box in 2075 they'll know what it was like nearly *two* hundred years ago, let alone one!"

"Here, steady on," said Gramma. "Not a hundred I'm not, thank you. Remember when bread was a penny a loaf I can, though."

"That's kind o' thing," Lizzie nodded. "And we're doing countryside as well—map on it, wi' all hedges and trees and footpaths marked. And wild flowers—all got a field each to do, and we're to pick flowers, see, and press 'em, and—"

"Flowers?" interrupted Patty. "Flowers'll be same in a hundred years as they are now." She laughed. "Daisies look same to me now as they did when I was a kid, any road."

"But there might not *be* any daisies," said Lizzie, half enjoying the drama of such a statement, half horrorstruck at the very idea of its possibly being true.

Patty stared at her, then laughed again, evidently having decided it could not be true.

"'S'true! Miss Platt says it's all the spraying and that. She says if any of us find a hedgerow wi' more than fourteen kinds of wild flower in it, we're to tell her, and she'll have it preserved."

"Preserved?" echoed Patty. To her, things that were preserved were in bottles, like greengage jam. And she could not picture a bottled hedgerow, quite.

"Kept," explained Lizzie. "Protected, like. Nobody let go spraying it, and that. Jonathan's helping me. Not that he's much help. Hardly knows a celandine from a buttercup, he doesn't. . . ."

Jonathan sprawled in the long hot grass while Lizzie herself was kneeling in it. She examined the clover carefully, because what she really wanted was a four-leafed one. The sun burned into her skin, the cuckoo called and Lizzie thought: "Wish I could put today in the tin box wi' a label on it: 'July 14th, 1975'. Wish I could put the whole thing in—sun, cuckoo, smells and all."

Unconsciously she stretched out her arms in a vain attempt to draw the whole thing together, embrace it. The woods on the skyline shimmered in the heat and Lizzie could even imagine the coolness inside there in the green light under the trees and the ker-ker of comfortable, well-fed pigeons and the drone of summer flies in ferns.

"Could take a *photo*, I s'pose," she thought. "That might do it."

She took the polaroid camera she had been given last Christmas and peered through the lens, trying to find the view that would tell best how it had been on this particular summer day in 1975. Lizzie heard the shutter click, withdrew the film and tucked it under her arm while it developed.

A minute later she was looking at it, and knew at once that she had failed. The view was there, right enough, but something was missing, some all-important quality whose absence made the photograph a mere— photograph. Lizzie sighed.

"Pity," she murmured aloud.

"What?" Jonathan's eyes were closed and he was sucking at a long grass.

"Pity you can't put *real* things in a box to keep. I mean, 's'all right putting price of eggs, and how Gramma won Sunday School prize when she was little. But when they open it, in 2075, I don't reckon it'll *tell* 'em anything. Not really."

"So what do you want to put in?" enquired Jonathan, eyes still shut. "A piece of birthday cake?"

Lizzie looked down at him.

"Not a bad idea, that's not," she told him. Then she looked back at the landscape spellbound in the heat.

"Today. That's what I'd put in if I could. How it *feels*."

Jonathan opened his eyes, squinting into the sun.

"They'll still have days like this," he said. "Bound to, even in 2075."

"Not exactly," said Lizzie, certain of it. "Never be a day again *exactly* like today. Even we'll never have one exactly the same. 'Cos *we'll* be different, see."

"Oh, well!" Jonathan spat out the grass, picked another, then lay back and shut his eyes again. "Wish we could get done wi' the wild flowers and get on wi't *interviewing*. I'm going to do Aunt Blodwen."

Lizzie giggled.

"Pity posterity! They'll not believe in her. They'll think you made her up!"

"Who're you doing?"

"Mam. Dad. Gramma. Mrs Adams, I might."

"Nobody very interesting much, is there? Not *really* interesting."

The idea came to Lizzie then, ravishing in its power and simplicity.

"The witch!"

She must have said the word out loud.

"The—what?"

Lizzie was silent.

"Did you say *witch*?"

"I've a good mind to tell him," she thought.

"You did, didn't you?" he persisted. "You said it once before, as well. What d'ye mean, witch?"

Lizzie looked at him then, straight in the eyes.

"I mean—witch," she said.

It had been said at last. He sat up.

"Witch?" he said. "Witch? You're barmy."

"Oh, I know," agreed Lizzie, hiding her disappointment. "Nobody believes a single word I say. Didn't you know?"

She stood up.

"Where're you going?"

"You wouldn't believe me if I told you," she answered, and began to run.

"Hey! Lizzie!"

She took no notice. Clutching her wild flowers in one hand and the camera in the other she went pell-mell down the green lane between the high, scented hedgerows and white sprays.

> "Lizzie Dripping, Lizzie Dripping,
>   Don't look now your fibs are slipping!"

She stopped and looked back. All was still. There was no sign of pursuit.

"Shouldn't've told him," she thought. "Wish I hadn't."

She walked on slowly. "Thing is, they won't believe it in 2075 either," she thought. "If they don't believe me now, wi't witch just round't corner, they never will *then*...."

Another idea came, quite effortlessly. She lifted the polaroid camera and stared at it as if it were magic as any witch's spell.

"Ooh ... warrif ... ?" A photograph of a real witch, sitting on a real tombstone! Her witch, caught forever in the lens, inescapably a fact, for people in Little Hemlock

now, let alone in 2075.

"I will!" she thought exultantly. "I'll do it! *Have* to believe in her then, they would—*and* that Jonathan, *and* the rest on 'em! Oooh—why didn't I think of it afore?"

And Lizzie Dripping started to run again.

Five minutes later she was behind the east wall of the church.

"Better not let her see camera," she thought. And then, "What's it matter? Won't know what it is, even if she *do* see it. Look funny, standing wi' hands behind me back. Just swing it—careless like. She won't know what it is...."

She practised swinging the camera carelessly for a moment, then advanced.

"Do interview first," she thought, "then take photo at end. Might get mad, else."

A very small voice right at the back of Lizzie's head was telling her not to do either, either the interview or the photograph. But Lizzie was bent on securing that tricky witch *now*, for ever more, tying her down, pinning her like a butterfly. She pretended she did not hear the warning voice. She edged round the corner of the church, cautious even after so many meetings and so many conversations. The witch was there. She sat perfectly still, her eyes closed, looking curiously blissful and at peace.

"Asleep?" Lizzie wondered. "Not sitting *up*!"

"Witch!" she called softly. "It's me—Lizzie!"

The witch gave a long, soft sigh and opened her eyes, reluctantly it seemed, looking dazed and far away.

"Doing a spell, were you?" Lizzie was awestruck by the very thought.

The witch nodded.

"I was—somewhere else," she said.

"Somewhere else? Just now? How?"

"Easy," said the witch. "Shut your eyes and be where you will. Easy, girl. Child's play."

"I s'pose it is," agreed Lizzie slowly. "For anyone really, not just witches. If you shut your eyes, *anything* can happen."

"That's right," said the witch. "You'll learn. You'll learn, my deary."

"Called me deary!" thought Lizzie. "Never done *that* afore! Try her now, straight off, I'd better...."

"Witch," she said aloud, "d'ye think ... can I ask you some questions? Just a few?"

"Questions?" All at once the witch was on guard again. "What kind of questions?"

"A sort of an interview," said Lizzie. "For a project we're doing at school. It'd not take long."

"Go on, then," said the witch surprisingly. One way or another she was being very surprising today. "Ask one. Not saying I'll answer, mind."

"Oh thank you!" cried Lizzie. "Thank you!"

She sat down then, with her back leaning against the comfortable tomb of Betsy Mabel Glossop, aged 79 years (*Life's Work Well Done*). She fished out her pencil

and notebook and was ready, pencil poised. The camera lay by her right side in the grass.

"I know I've asked you this afore," she began then, "but I really would like to know. What your *name* is."

"Not telling!" snapped the witch instantly. "What else?"

"Well, I—I don't s'pose you'd tell me—how old you are?"

The witch threw back her head then and cackled. She went on cackling and screaming for so long it seemed as though she would never stop. When at last she did, she fixed Lizzie with a glittering stare and chanted: "Time is now and time is then and time is soon and time is for ever and ever! For ever and ever!"

She flung out her arms with the last words as if she were actually holding time in her skinny palms, and scattering it like cold corn to the winds. Poor Lizzie sat nonplussed.

"And wherever time is," went on the witch, "there am I."

"So—so you'll still be here in a hundred years' time, then," asked Lizzie, trying to work it all out. "In 2075?"

"I already am," crooned the witch, smug and enigmatic. "I already am!"

"Oh," said Lizzie. "Oh."

She wrote in her notebook: *Is already in 2075.*

"Waste o' time, asking her questions," she thought. But she had to try once more. Her next question was one she hardly knew how to ask, hardly *dared* to ask, even. It was one she desperately wanted the answer to, not only for posterity's sake, but for her own. She swallowed.

"Witch," she began, "witch, don't get mad, will you . . . ?"

The witch did not reply. She sat and hugged herself and rocked, and watched Lizzie.

"What I wanted to know is—well, what I wondered is—are you *real*? Oh, *I* believe in you, I do. What I mean is, if it's just *me* that sees you, you might not be *really* real, see. More like a kind of a dream or summat."

She stopped. She knew that she had said it all badly. The witch sat and rocked on her wide stone slab and said not a word.

"*Are* you? Please witch—*please*?"

"She ain't going to say owt," Lizzie thought. "Oh, *why* won't she tell! Oh—I know!"

She suddenly remembered the camera and realised that she could force an answer of sorts, and quick as thought snatched up the camera, raised it, caught the witch in the lens and—click!

Lizzie lowered the camera.

"Gone! Oh quick—film!"

She pulled out the film and tucked it under her arm. Part of her mind was counting seconds, part racing with questions one after another.

"Gone! Why? For ever? Was it what I said? Was it—this?"

She drew out the film and peeled away the skin. She hardly dared to look. A gasp flew from her lips.

The photograph had come out well. It showed, black and white, the sun-flecked tomb of the Perfectly Peaceful Posts, the overhanging tree, the tall and whitening summer grass. What it did not show, not even as a smudge, not even as the merest blur, was a witch. For Lizzie, the shock had the force of a spell.

"Gone!"

The word, said out loud, was more bleak and true than it had ever seemed before. Lizzie looked down at the hateful photograph and back at the empty tomb and knew that she had betrayed her witch. By trying to make her real, she had made her unreal, had sent her into a silence and invisibility that might last for ever now.

"Oh witch!" Lizzie was close to tears. "I'm sorry, I'm sorry! Look!"

And she held up the photograph and tore it right
across, then again and again.

There was no reply. Lizzie stared at the empty tombs
and shivered because she thought she knew now that
never would she look into those sour green eyes again,
never hear that high cackle, see those stabbing white
fingers. The witch had gone from Little Hemlock.
The air, once thick with flying spells, was empty now,
ordinary air for breathing.

"I *am* Lizzie Dripping," she thought dully. "They're
right. I am. . . ."

And Lizzie walked away.

". . . ever so many other things. Ever so many."

Lizzie lifted her head, came out of her dreaming. Aunt
Blodwen was only a few yards in front of her, talking to
Miss Platt over her garden hedge.

"Hello, Lizzie," called Miss Platt, and smiled.

"Hello, Miss Platt."

"Oh—Lizzie Dripping, is it! Where's Jonathan? With you, I thought, picking flowers."

"Oh, he was," Lizzie said. "Still is, for all I know."

"How are you getting on, Lizzie?" asked Miss Platt. "I'm collecting so many things it looks as if there'll have to be half a dozen boxes, not just one."

"Oh yes, I was telling you, Miss Pratt," began Aunt Blodwen eagerly.

"Platt," corrected Lizzie and Miss Platt together.

"Platt—ever so many things. Me and Arthur on our wedding day—definitely let you have a photo of that, though I must say I like my hair better the style I've got it now. And then there's one of me taken at the seaside, judging a competition, would you believe, right next to the Mayor. Half a dozen photos of that I've got—in the newspapers it was, and my name on it and all."

56

"Why, thank you, Mrs Cole," said Miss Platt. "That would be nice."

"Well—thought it'd be something a bit different, see!" Aunt Blodwen gave a deprecating little laugh. "Can't imagine why they picked on me—all those thousands as there were—but there you are. Picked me right out from among them all and next thing I knew there I was right next to the Mayor and heaven knows! Wasn't I, Lizzie? Lizzie!"

Lizzie nodded grudgingly.

"Lovely," said Miss Platt.

"Mind, lovely idea of yours, Miss Pratt," said Aunt Blodwen. "Just to fancy—people in a hundred years' time to see that silly old photo of me with the Mayor! There *is* a photo somewhere of the flower arrangement in an egg cup I won first prize with at Mapleburn—1967 I think it was. Not one of my best, I thought. Bit limiting an egg cup, see. But there you are. I expect the judges knew best."

"Just hark at her," thought Lizzie. "Tin box to *herself* she'll want, afore she's done. Put her in a tin box, that's what I'd like, egg cups and all."

She started to walk off.

"Lizzie!" Miss Platt called after her, and she turned.

"Call round some time if you like, and see all the things I've collected. You could help me decide which to put in."

Lizzie nodded.

"Thanks. Yes, Miss Platt, I'd like that."

At the corner of Wellow Lane was a little group, who turned and watched her approach. Jonathan was among them.

"Lizzie Dripping, Lizzie Dripping!"

"Who believes in witches, then?"

"Look out, Lizzie Dripping—*witch*'ll get you— whooooeeeee!"

"Seen any witches lately? Look out—there's one behind you!"

"Oh, shut up, shut up!" cried Lizzie. "Let me alone!"

"Who believes in witches? Lizzie Dripping!"

"I don't, I don't!" she cried. "Let me alone. I don't, I tell you!"

She began to run, and hardly heard their voices following, and felt the tears run hot on her cheeks. At last she slowed down and brushed her arm across her eyes and thought "I do I do I do!" and beyond that thought was an echo of a thought: "You don't you don't you don't!"

During the days that followed Lizzie was always hearing that voice and always trying to prove it wrong. She went to the graveyard (despite Patty's warnings) three and sometimes four times a day. Even on wet days she went, and would crouch under the dry yew by the Posts' tomb till her knees ached and she felt queer and giddy from staring into the falling rain. She went out of a blind and dogged obstinacy, because Lizzie Dripping was not going to see that witch ever again. She knew it without needing to prove it, and yet was determined to prove it.

"I never said goodbye, even," she would think suddenly in the middle of doing a jigsaw or walking along on quite an ordinary errand. And straightaway she would go on searching again, sometimes to the graveyard, sometimes to the mill, the Larkins' pond—anywhere in Little Hemlock where once that witch had been. She even went to the ten-acre and tried her own spell again:

> "Witch appear, witch appear,
> I make you witch, out of the air!"

Time and again she said the words, time and again she plucked vainly at daisies—"witch, not, witch, not . . ." And more than once she cried herself to sleep.

It was after a visit to the graveyard that she saw Miss Platt in her garden again, and was invited in to see the growing hoard of treasure for the tin box. On a table covered with a fringed red plush cloth they were arranged in tidy groups, every item numbered and

entered in a stiff covered notebook.

"It almost makes you wish you could be there yourself when the box is opened," said Miss Platt. "Can't you imagine how excited they'll be? It makes me wish *we* had one to open. And the different things we've collected! Look at this."

"What is it?" Lizzie took the photograph.

"It's the first car in Little Hemlock. Mrs Draycott gave it, at the Post Office—it belonged to her father. And you know what *this* is, of course." She held out another picture.

"Us!" said Lizzie. "On that footpath walk! There's Gramma! Eeeh—and look at me—mouth stuffed full— will they really see *me* then, in 2075? Funniest feeling it gives you, don't it? We'll all be *dead*—even me—even Toby! It's not morbid to say that, is it, Miss Platt? It's true, anyhow. But Mam says it's morbid—*and* going into't graveyard."

She stared gloomily at the picture in her hand and thought again, inevitably, of the witch and that other ill-fated photograph.

"Is something the matter, Lizzie?" asked Miss Platt.

"Oooh," Lizzie hesitated. "I wish I could tell you."

"And can't you?"

"You'd laugh. They all do."

"I don't think I would. In fact, I'm sure I wouldn't."

"Even if you didn't laugh you'd think I was a fibber," said Lizzie bitterly. "Everyone does. There's *nobody* I can tell, not in the whole world."

"It really is a secret, then?"

Lizzie nodded.

"I wonder—I wonder if it has anything to do with a witch?"

"A—how do you know?" Lizzie gasped.

Miss Platt laughed then.

"I'm not deaf, Lizzie. I think I already know that you go and meet a witch in the graveyard."

"And—and you believe me?"

"I think, Lizzie," said Miss Platt carefully, "that people's witches are their own affair. I don't for a single minute think that if *I* went to the graveyard I would meet your witch. Or that anyone else would, for that matter—except you."

Lizzie, to her dismay, felt tears springing.

"Only I don't see her any more!" she cried. At last she was able to tell. "Oh Miss Platt—she's gone, gone for ever. I know she has, and it's all my fault! And that old witch, she was smashing, she was . . . oh!"

And now Lizzie began to sob in earnest.

"My friend, she was! And then I went and took a photo of her—wanted to prove she was there, see, really there, so's th'others wouldn't laugh at me!"

"And she wasn't there," said Miss Platt. "At least, she didn't show on the photograph."

Lizzie looked up.

"Didn't show? You mean—she could've been real and

still not showed on photo?"

Miss Platt nodded. "That's exactly what I mean, Lizzie. I believe she was real—to you."

"True, that is," said Lizzie. "Aye, that's true. But what I really wanted was to put her in't box, see, for 2075. So's *they'd* know about her."

"Ah—I see. Well, I think we can do something about that."

"But what? She don't *come* any more—I've been there dozens o' times—and to't mill, *and* to't pond."

"How do you know about witches, Lizzie?" asked Miss Platt surprisingly. "How did you know what one looked like, for instance, before you met your own?"

"Know? Well—I—from books, I s'pose."

"That's right. That's how we all know. So you see there *is* a way you can tell them about your witch in 2075."

"*Is* there?"

"Listen. Tomorrow is the first day of term. And in the afternoon I'm going to ask you all to sing one or two songs—and one of them, as a matter of fact, is one *about* witches—the one we learned last term. And I'm going to record them, and then put the tape in the tin trunk. So what we'll do, is this. . . ."

Next day Lizzie left school half-an-hour early, the cassette recorder in her satchel.

"Lizzie is leaving early because she's doing something for me," Miss Platt had told the others. "Something special, for the 2075 box."

And the rest of them were still singing, Lizzie could hear their voices following, singing about witches:

"Oooooh! Oooh!
We crouch on Pendle Hill
When all the moors are still,
We feed on roots and moory moss and shale;
We weave our spells of spite
All through the creeping night
And skip and dance like scarecrows in a gale!"

Lizzie was making for the graveyard.

"Rather do it there," she had told Miss Platt. "It'll seem more—more real. And anyhow, if that old witch hears me, she might—well, you never know."

"You'll be making her real anyhow," Lizzie thought now. "Miss Platt says so. *And* she'll be real to them that hears the tape in a hundred years."

She went into the graveyard and climbed the familiar steep pathway into the sky and walked down by the side of the church, not slowly or with caution as once she had, because she did not expect to meet the witch now.

She chose a place to sit under the yew, so that as she told her story she could see the tomb of the Perfectly Peaceful Posts. There she sat quietly for a moment or two drawing in the dry, woody smell, seeing the way the glinting ivy curled and remembering meetings, hearing voices.

"Where shall I begin?" she wondered, and placed the cassette recorder in the grass. "Right at the beginning, I·s'pose, tell 'em who I am first. 'Once upon a time'— aye, that's how they always start. . . ."

Lizzie picked up the microphone, pressed the button marked "record", and began:

"Once upon a time—and I mean last week, or last year—there was a girl called Lizzie Dripping. . . ."

And so Lizzie began her story, and before long the witch was there again in her mind's eye, hunched and mocking and dusty and in some curious way more there, more Lizzie's, than ever before.

". . . Lizzie saw the witch before the witch saw her. What the witch was doing, was sitting with her back propped against a tombstone—the one in memory of Hannah Post of this parish and Albert Cyril beloved husband of the above 1802 to 1879 Peace Perfect Peace. . . ."

It was a very long time before Lizzie had finished her story. She heard the church clock strike six and knew she had missed tea and did not even care. She stopped the tape, thought for a moment, and then started it again.

"And this is a true story," she said loudly and firmly. "Signed—Lizzie Dripping!"

Then she pressed the button that said *Stop*, got up, and began to walk away down the pathway from the sky.